Grandpa Loved

BY
JOSEPHINE NOBISSO

ILLUSTRATED BY
MAUREEN HYDE

The Green Tiger Press, Inc.
San Diego
1989

Text copyright © 1989 by Josephine Nobisso
Illustrations copyright © 1989 by Maureen Hyde
The Green Tiger Press
ISBN 0-88138-119-5
2 4 6 8 10 9 7 5 3
Library of Congress Card Catalog No.88-83403
Manufactured in Hong Kong

To Grandpa Ralph and his four girls:
Nicolle, Gina, Bianca, and Kali Marie
—J.N.

For my father, with special thanks
to Russ, Jake and Sam.
—M.H.

Grandpa loved to stand on the beach.
He showed me how to love it, too.

We let the ocean foam creep up our legs, and the sun squint our eyes. We let the sea air breathe us—in and out, in and out—very deeply, very friendly. Inside us, the brine tingled.

Grandpa said that the earth was hurtling through space so fast that it sent winds across the planet.

That's what he loved most about the beach—being the tallest thing and catching all that wind.

Grandpa loved the woods behind the summer house. He planted that love in me too.

We lay in beds of soft moist moss, and tunneled into drifts of dry leaves.

We built a manger where deer and rabbits and raccoons came to eat our bread and corn and garden greens. Grandpa said that the woodland creatures are so gentle and sensitive that they feel any fear or nervousness around them.

That's what Grandpa loved most about the woods—being so calm and easy with all those animals.

Grandpa loved the city where we live. He taught me to love it, too. We let the dusty warm scent in museums carry us away, and the quiet buzz of the library lull us to doze, like lazy flies.

We let any lost and lonely person tell us a life's story. Grandpa said that his being so old, and my being so young, made it easy for people to tell us so much.

That's what Grandpa loved most about the city—being so old and hearing all those lives.

Grandpa loved the people in our family.
He grew that love in me, too.

We danced at weddings, and sang at parties. We played with the new babies, and visited the sick.

Grandpa said that people who died could go anywhere and see anything at all. That must be what Grandpa likes most about not being here anymore—being with us everywhere, all the time—in the wind, in the creatures, and in the lives of all who loved him.